Camel Ben

a limerick

by Carter Boucher
illustrated by Bruce MacDonald

Richard C. Owen Publishers, Inc.
Katonah, New York

There was a tall camel named Ben.

3

He tripped and fell
now and then.

5

He fell off a wall

and had a great fall.

Now instead of one hump
he has ten.